GW00738150

THOMAS HARDY
AND THE
JURASSIC COAST

A guide compiled by
Patrick Tolfree and Rebecca Welshman
Illustrations by David Brackston

Published by The Thomas Hardy Society

The Society is grateful for the support of the
County Council's Jurassic Coast Trust in producing this guide

The Society would like to thank David Brackston
for his generosity in providing illustrations
for Thomas Hardy and the Jurassic Coast

Acknowledgements to the Dorchester County Museum
for photographs reproduced from the Thomas Hardy archive

ISBN: 978-0-9566370-0-0

 Printed by Creeds Telephone: **01308 423411** Web: **www.creedsuk.com**

Contents

INTRODUCTION

By Dr Tony Fincham
Chairman of the Thomas Hardy Society

O the opal and the sapphire of that wandering western sea,
And the woman riding high above with bright hair flapping free –
The woman whom I loved so, and who loyally loved me.
('Beeny Cliff' [291])

The sea is an essential ingredient in the magic mixture which inspired Hardy's creative writings - time and again both his poetic persona and his fictional protagonists turn towards that 'wild weird western shore' and the magnificent scenery of the Dorset coastline whose tumultuous perspectives so often serve as analogies for the tumultuous upheavals in their lives and loves. Hardy's Wessex is bounded by an enchanted shoreline – the majesty and mystery of which has recently achieved international recognition in its designation as The Jurassic Coast World Heritage Site. The term 'Jurassic' was first coined by Lyell in the 1830s to refer to geological formations composed primarily of oolitic limestone as in the Jura mountains; although Hardy never used the word Jurassic in his writings, he referred repeatedly to the oolitic limestone of the Isle of Slingers so he can be seen as a Jurassic Coast man from the start.

The guide brings together Dorset's two main claims to world-wide fame, namely its natural heritage, which records 185 million years of the earth's ancient history in just 95 miles of undulating coastline, and its literary heritage, the author and poet of Shakespearean stature and durability who was born in a cob-and-thatch cottage on the edge of an obscure heath within a short walk of the throb of those 'hill-hid tides'. An author and poet whose writings focussed again and again on the relationship between man and his environment, man and his fellow creatures, man against geological time, man against the stellar universe – he was a child of Dorset's natural heritage - and his poetry and fiction offer us - the children of a more distant century – the opportunity to understand the natural heritage which surrounds us and on which we depend for our survival.

The authors have worked tirelessly to produce this guide on behalf of The Thomas Hardy Society and in conjunction with the Jurassic Coast Trust – both educational charities committed to promoting knowledge and understanding of Dorset's - and England's - unique heritage. Allow this book to open 'the door of the West' for you

> With its loud sea-lashings,
> And cliff-side clashings
> Of waters rife with revelry.
>> ('She Opened the Door' [740])

PREFACE

In December 2001 the entirety of the Dorset coastline, and that of East Devon, now popularly known as 'The Jurassic Coast', was identified by the United Nations Educational, Scientific and Cultural Organisation (UNESCO) as a World Heritage Site. This means that the area, a distance of 95 miles, is deemed to be of 'outstanding universal value'. Formed as a result of geological events and coastal processes the unique formations allow insight into 185 million years of earth's history, and span the Jurassic, Triassic, and Cretaceous periods.[1] The Jurassic Coast is significant as it is England's first natural World Heritage site while being one of only four such natural sites in the UK, and 174 worldwide.[2]

Rich in archaeology and palaeontology, as well as geology, the Dorset and Devon coastal area has attracted and inspired writers for centuries. Thomas Hardy, the Victorian author, described in the *Times* in 1910 as 'the greatest figure among living novelists',[3] lived most of his life within five miles of this remarkable heritage coastline.

In part one we consider the affinities between Hardy and the Jurassic Coast. In the second part we list twenty Hardy-Jurassic Coast landmarks, all of which are on, or within approximately five miles of, the World Heritage Site. A landmark may be a house, a village, a town, site of historic interest or a locality that is of importance either in Hardy's life or work, or both.

Thomas Hardy and the Jurassic Coast aims to broaden awareness of Hardy's affinity with the Dorset and Devon coastline, while encouraging readers to consider Hardy's life and work from a more scientifically and geographically informed perspective.

It will also, we hope, be useful to those who are planning walks in Hardy country. While there is a tendency to think of Hardy's Wessex solely or mainly in terms of the novels, the guide highlights the importance of the short stories and poetry to what Hardy called his 'half real, half-dream country.'

Sources

1. All quotations in the guide from Hardy's poetry are taken from *The Complete Poems of Thomas Hardy*, New Wessex Edition, edited by James Gibson, published by Macmillan in 1976. The number of the poem in that edition is shown in square brackets.

2. Other sources are given numerically in endnotes. Except where otherwise indicated, quotations from Hardy's novels and short stories are taken from the New Wessex Edition of Hardy's work, published by Macmillan (1912-13).

3. References to the *'Life'* are to *The Life and Work of Thomas Hardy*, by Thomas Hardy, edited by Professor Millgate and published by Macmillan in 1984.

ILLUSTRATIONS

* Scanned image and text by Philip V. Allingham: http://www.victorianweb.org/art/illustration/pasquier/6.html

PART ONE
HARDY AND THE JURASSIC COAST

The horizon gets lost in a mist new-wrought by the night:
    The lamps of the Bay
That reach from behind me round to the left and right
    On the sea-wall way
For a constant mile of curve, make a long display
    As a pearl-strung row,
Under which in the waves they bore their gimlets of light:-
    All this was plain; but there was a thing not so.
('On the Esplanade' [682])

Hardy: the Landscape and the Past

Hardy was born and died in Dorset, having spent seventy-three of his
eighty-seven years in the county of his birth. A number of his novels,
stories and poetry were written either at the Higher Bockhampton cottage
were he was born and grew up, or at Max Gate, the house on the outskirts
of Dorchester into which he moved with his first wife, Emma Gifford,
in 1885. Those two places are, respectively, six and five miles from the
Dorset coast, as the crow flies.

The majority of Hardy's fiction is set in the south west of the country,
for which he adopted the name of Wessex (originally the kingdom of the
West Saxons). Hardy liked to be able to visualise in his mind's eye the
settings of his novels and stories and a powerful sense of place imbues his
work. A large number of the locations he used in his fiction, many with
fictional names, are also within five or so miles of the sea. Hardy is one of
many authors who have used the Jurassic Coast as a setting*, and he was
fully aware of the imaginative possibilities afforded by placing stories of

---

* Other well known authors who have based their work in and around the Jurassic Coast include
Jane Austen, John Fowles, and John Betjeman.

human life within the grander sequence of geological time.

Although Hardy's world was largely agricultural, there is also a distinctively maritime content in his work that counterbalances the themes of mechanisation, rural community, and the barrenness of Egdon Heath. The threat of Bonaparte invading the Dorset coast was for Hardy a living memory. The war with France provides the setting for his novel *The Trumpet-Major*, and features in different ways elsewhere in his fiction and in his epic verse-drama *The Dynasts*. There are short stories of Hardy's which incorporate smuggling, the Newfoundland fishing trade, rope-making and quarrying. In Hardy's novel, *The Well-Beloved*, 'Vindilia' (the Roman name for Portland) is the predominant setting, described by Hardy as 'the peninsula carved by Time out of a single stone'.

Hardy's powerful sense of place is reinforced by an equally powerful sense of the past. Dorchester and the surrounding area are rich in Roman and pre-Roman remains, including Maiden Castle, Maumbury Rings, Poundbury Hill Fort and the Roman Town House. Hardy grew up aware of Dorchester's rich heritage. From the age of ten he walked every day to school through what had been the Town Centre of Dorchester since Roman times. Hardy absorbed the past through his feet. He also grew up aware of the success as a fossil-hunter of Mary Anning of Lyme Regis whose fame had spread far beyond Dorset by the mid nineteenth century. When Hardy was 43 he returned to Dorchester and purchased, from the Duchy of Cornwall, the plot of land on which he built Max Gate. In the course of laying the foundations several skeletons, dating from the Romano-British era, were discovered in three separate graves.

The visible antiquity of the heritage coastline inspired Hardy's interest in past ages. That nineteenth-century geology afforded insight into times that were both 'grand' and 'mean' in terms of their relics was, for Hardy, a fascinating and intriguing concept. After the mid-Victorian scientific breakthroughs of geologist Charles Lyell, and Charles Darwin's theory of evolution, the significance of human life within the context of earth's history underwent a dramatic reassessment. The publication of Sir John Lubbock's *Prehistoric Times* in 1872, the same year in which Hardy's novel *A Pair of Blue Eyes* was published in serial form in *Tinsley's Magazine*,

Hardy at the time of his marriage to Emma Gifford © Dorset County Museum.

was part of a new phase of scientific study known as prehistory which focussed on life before the time of written records. The way that Hardy placed characters in close affinity with their landscapes was part of a late-nineteenth century exploratory trend that sought to represent scientific thought as tangible and accessible. The imaginative use of geological and archaeological settings afforded a new form of literary space in which to explore the complex relations between past and present.

The Victorians and the Jurassic Coast

The coastline of Dorset and south Devon was well known in the early Victorian era for its stone, fossils, and seafaring stories. During the procurement of materials such as Purbeck marble and Portland stone accidental discovery of fossil remains led to increasing scientific interest in the stretch of coast between Swanage and Exeter.

Mary Anning of Lyme Regis was the first to discover a complete *Icthyosaur* fossil. This discovery was followed by a *Plesiosaur,* and then the first flying reptile, known as Dimorphodon, a kind of *Pterodactyl.* The impact of Mary Anning on Victorians' appreciation of the Jurassic Coast was equal to that of her contemporary, Jane Austen, who is known for her timeless portrayal of Lyme Regis in her novel *Persuasion.* Hardy's own work recognises the popularisation of the Jurassic Coast during the previous century, and he often uses the coast as a setting for the more dramatic moments in his novels, as well a place of meditative reflection in his poetry. The paleonotological discoveries associated with Lyme Regis and its environs connected the Dorset and Devon coast with the scientific movement in London and with other paleonotological sites around the world, and this is something that the young, socially aspiring Thomas Hardy, would have appreciated.

One early dinosaur enthusiast was Queen Victoria's husband, Prince Albert. He often attended the naturalist Richard Owen's lectures and in 1852 encouraged Owen to create an outdoor exhibit of prehistoric creatures to be displayed at Sydenham Park, London (see illustration on the following page). The Albert Memorial Museum in Exeter was built in 1865 to honour Albert's interests in palaeontology and geology.

The museum was a place that Hardy visited, and the exhibit of a cast of a skeleton labelled "Archaeopteryx macrura. The oldest fossil bird. Upper Jurassic Lithographic Stone, Solenhafen, Bavaria"[4] was to be the inspiration for Hardy's poem 'In a Museum' [358]. The *Life* records that on June 10, 1915, he "Motored with F[lorence] to Bridport, Lyme, Exeter, and Torquay ... Then back to Teignmouth, Dawlish, and Exeter, putting up at the 'Clarence' opposite the Cathedral".[5]

Sydenham Park Sculptures

The railway reached Weymouth in 1857, when Hardy was 17, accommodating both the Great Western Railway and the London and South Western Railway. Brighton, Bournemouth and Weymouth experienced renewed interest from Londoners wishing to holiday by the sea – a level of interest not seen since the heyday of the Regency period the century before. Portland became accessible by rail in 1865 when a custom made wooden bridge was built across Radipole Lake. During the time that Hardy lived in London he would have easily been able to travel to the coast.

In the *Life* Hardy attributes the loss of traditional rural ballad songs being sung at rural celebrations to the extension of the railway line to Dorchester. The direct connection to London meant the final bridging of the physical and cultural distance between rural Dorset and the more built-up south of England. As Hardy phrases it, the 'orally transmitted ditties of centuries [were] slain at a stroke by the London comic songs that were introduced.' Notably, Hardy's recollections of a harvest-supper at a local farm that he attended when he was ten recall a particular ballad set on the Scottish coast, called "The Western Tragedy".[6] Also known as 'May Colvin' the ballad depicts the plight of a resourceful woman who evades the murderous intent of a treacherous man:

> Lie there, lie there, thou false-hearted man,
> Lie there instead o' me;
> For six pretty maidens thou hast a-drown'd here,
> But the seventh hath drown-ed thee!

This, says Hardy, was probably one of the last times that this ballad was sung at such an event before the new transport connection with London altered the ballad tradition for good.

Many of the Hardy landmarks which we have identified on and around the Jurassic Coast are visible from one another. The view, for example, from the Iron Age Hillfort, Pilsdon Pen, encompasses the majority of the Jurassic Coast, and the view from West Bay, Bridport, affords generous views to the east - of Weymouth and Portland - and views west to Branscombe and Sidmouth. One of Hardy's favourite pastimes was cycling. Hardy once told his friend, Sir George Douglas, that when cycling, 'you can go out a long distance without coming in contact with another mind, - not even a horse's – and dissipating any little mental energy that has arisen in the course of a morning's application.'[7] It is likely that Hardy would have visited some of the more inaccessible landmarks, such as Netherbury and Wynyard's Gap, by bicycle and would have had time to appreciate the extensive views across to the coast. His poetry, especially during the 1890's when he was known to take long cycling trips alone, certainly suggests a combined appreciation of the geographic location and the archaeological and geological significance of the Jurassic Coast area. During the winter of 1897-8 Hardy embarked upon a series of expeditions along the coast in preparation for the architectural illustrations in *Wessex Poems*. At East Lulworth he made some technical reports on a church in need of restoration for the Society for the Protection of Ancient Buildings. Professor Michael Millgate, Hardy's principal biographer, suggests that quite possibly Hardy ventured further along the coast to the Kimmeridge coast-guard's cottage where his early love Eliza Nicholl's once lived. In 'Winter Words' opposite the first of the four 'She to Him' poems [14], Hardy inserted his sketch which shows a male and female figure, walking or standing hand in hand on a path that leads up towards a building indentifiable as Clavel Tower.[8]

For all its rugged beauty the Dorset coast represented a landscape imbued with tragedy and danger. From the erosive and unpredictable tides which had shipwrecked sailing vessels through the centuries, to the more imminent exposure of the southern coast to foreign attack, the Dorset coastline was a challenging and inspiring setting; one that was certainly not overlooked by Hardy.

Hardy's 'cliff-hanger'

A well known episode in Hardy's novel, *A Pair of Blue Eyes*, published in 1873, illustrates particularly well Hardy's kinship with the past and the imaginative dimension that geology and prehistory gave to his writing. In the book Hardy suggests there is a link between the material presence of coastal landscapes, which develop gradually over time, and the human response to landscape that is often sudden and spontaneous.

'On the Cliffs'

Knight and his fiancée, Elfride Swancourt, are walking on the cliffs – 'a vast stratification of blackish-gray slate' – when Knight loses his hat in a sudden gust of wind. In his endeavour to retrieve the hat, Knight descends the slope that leads to the great cliff. Softened by the sudden onset of rain, the slope becomes treacherous and Knight loses his footing, held only by 'a bracket of quartz rock, standing out like a tooth from the verge of the precipice.' Elfride moves swiftly to help him, but becomes stuck herself.

In assisting Elfride, Knight slips further and saves himself by grabbing hold of a tuft of sea-pink. It would take Elfride three-quarters of an hour to fetch help and Knight estimates that, at the most, he has strength enough to hang on for ten minutes. He can only see Elfride's agonised face above him over the edge of the precipice, and then she disappears from view.

Suspended between life and death Knight experiences an intense few moments of evolutionary understanding and insight:

> By one of those familiar conjunctions of things wherewith the inanimate world baits the mind of man when he pauses in moments of suspense, opposite Knight's eyes was an imbedded fossil, standing forth in low relief from the rock. It was a creature with eyes. The eyes, dead and turned in stone, were even now regarding him. It was one of the early crustaceans called Trilobites*. Separated by millions of years in their lives, Knight and this underling seemed to have met in their place of death. It was the single instance within reach of his vision of anything that had ever been alive and had had a body to save, as he himself had now.

Hardy goes on to describe how Knight comes 'face to face with the beginning and all the intermediate centuries simultaneously.' He momentarily forgets his dire predicament in contemplation of aeons of past life, which 'passed before [his] Inner eye in less than half a minute.' When Elfride returns she is carrying 'a bundle of white linen'. In her few minutes of absence Elfride had removed her underclothes with the intention of making a rope to assist her stranded fiancée. Only Hardy could imagine such a provocative and ingenious solution to Knight's predicament. This early suggestion of his interest in feminine courage and the position of women in society became a theme that Hardy explored further in his work, in particular the 1891 novel, *Tess of the D'Urbervilles*.

---

* See image reproduced on rear cover.

Hardy was in his early thirties when he wrote *A Pair of Blue Eyes*, which was his third novel. The cliff-hanger episode shows that at an early stage in his writing career Hardy had significant knowledge and understanding of geology as well as an imaginative awareness of, and insights into, prehistory. The February instalment of the serial in *Tinsleys' Magazine* ends with Elfride disappearing from view and Knight is left 'in the presence of a personalised loneliness.' The reader had to wait in suspense for a month before discovering that Knight was to be saved.

It was not until the popularisation of serialised adventure films in the early twentieth century that the term "cliff-hanger" was first used to describe the suspense in which viewers were left between episodes.[9] It is possible that Hardy's description of Knight's adventure was an early prototype "cliff-hanger", and his use of the device is likely to have contributed to its later popularisation.

Hardy and Portland

Hardy's desire to align imaginative human experience with the material reality of the coastal landscape is most poignantly addressed in *The Well-Beloved*, the last of his novels, published in serial form in 1893, and later in book form in 1897. In this novel, mostly set on Portland, Hardy combines his knowledge of archaeology and geology of the Portland area with his interest in the Platonic Ideal of romantic love.

The Island-bred sculptor Pierston is described as a 'native of natives' – suggesting that the character's inherited identification with the landscape is stronger within the Jurassic Coast region than it had been for characters in Hardy's earlier and better-known novel *The Return of the Native*, set within Egdon Heath. The 'many embodiments' of Pierston's fantastical imagination are directly associated with the 'infinitely stratified walls of oolite.' As the human affinity with a landscape develops over time and is passed on through generations, albeit modified by evolutionary and cultural variants, so the character of a landscape, such as Portland, is sculpted and shaped by the changing chemical states of its rock, variations in weather and climate, and the human impact of quarrying. By the late nineteenth century it had been established that the clays and shale of the Portland area, used in prehistoric and Roman pottery manufacture, were unique for their strength and durability; a quality attributed to their slow stratified formation over many thousands of years.

The gradual accumulation of strata within the 'single rock' that is Portland is mirrored within the emotional make-up of Pierston, whose powerful native instinct causes him to search for the human embodiment of his illusive feeling that he terms his 'Well-Beloved'. Yet Pierston is aware that, like the nature of the sea itself, this embodiment can be fleeting, transient, and erosive to his, and others' emotional well being. Pierston refers to his love of beauty as something transcendental, beyond philosophical, and beyond his own conception:

> To his Well-Beloved he had always been faithful; but she had had many embodiments. Each individuality known as Lucy, Jane, Flora, Evangeline, or whatnot, had been merely a transient condition of her. He did not recognize this as an excuse or as a defence, but as a fact simply. Essentially she was perhaps of no tangible substance; a spirit, a dream, a frenzy, a conception, an aroma, an epitomized sex, a light of the eye, a parting of the lips. God only knew what she really was; Pierston did not. She was indescribable.[10]

Pierston's sculpted figurines of Greek and Roman goddesses are symbolic of his young emotional impulse to seek the embodiment of his desires. The figurines appear throughout the novel, akin to museum exhibits, contained to his London studio and dusted by Avice the Third. Creations of Pierston's father's own quarried Portland stone, these symbols become obsolete once Pierston reaches old age and finally marries.

In the novel Hardy refers to the character Avice Caro as an 'object' that belongs to the rock of Portland, inferring his awareness of the relation between the individual life and the material significance of the region over time. Knowledge of the importance of Kimmeridge shale and Kimmeridge clay, part of the sedimentary stratum of the Jurassic period, grew during the mid to late nineteenth century, when archaeologists such as Wake Smart identified excavated objects made from Kimmeridge material to be of Roman origin.[11] William Barnes, neighbour and mentor to Hardy, was one of the first to suggest that Kimmeridge coal money – small spherical pieces of polished shale - had not been used as money but were waste pieces from a lathe. Barnes contributed his views to the *Gentleman's Magazine* in 1839, stating that the discovery at Fordington Hill, Dorchester, of skeletons with a lathe-turned "amulet" and an armlet were "clearly that of a Romanised Briton".[12] During the 1840's Barnes instigated the beginnings of the Dorset Natural history and Antiquarian Field Club, to which Hardy was later to present a paper in 1884. In Hardy's *Well-Beloved*, Pierston's profession as a sculptor of Purbeck stone suggests that Hardy, writing from an archaeologically informed perspective, perceived significant continuity between the manufacturing and sculpting practice of Roman and nineteenth-century south-Dorset communities living and quarrying in the same area.

PART TWO
HARDY-JURASSIC COAST LANDMARKS

The landmarks below are divided into five sections in geographic order, from west to east. Hardy's fictional names are in italics.

I - EXMOUTH TO BRIDPORT

1. Topsham*. A large village, three miles south of Exeter on the river Exe, Topsham was the home of Hardy's first cousin, Tryphena Gale (née Sparks), from 1877 to 1890. Born in Puddletown, she was the sixth child of Maria, his mother's sister, and James Sparks.

Tryphena Sparks   **Hardy, aged 21**

---

* Images of Tryphena Sparks and Hardy © Dorchester County Museum.

When Hardy gave up his job as an architect in London in 1867 Tryphena was a lively, attractive sixteen-year old, and during the period in which he was making the difficult transition from architecture to full-time writing, he and Tryphena had a relationship. In the summer of 1869 he took lodgings in Weymouth whilst undertaking short-term projects for the architect, G.R.Crickmay. Tryphena was planning to go to teacher training college and Hardy was busy writing *Desperate Remedies*. There is considerable disagreement between biographers over how close they became and how much they meant to each other during this period, but most would agree that the affair ended in early 1870 when Tryphena began a two-year teacher training course at Stockwell, London. In March of that year Hardy was sent on an architectural assignment to St Juliot in Cornwall, where he met and fell in love with Emma Gifford, whom he married in 1874. On completion of her teacher training in 1872 Tryphena was appointed head of a girls' elementary school in Plymouth. In 1877 she married Charles Gale, a publican from Topsham, where they set up home and had four children. She died on March 17th, 1890, and is buried in Topsham cemetery.

After Tryphena left Dorset to go to college she disappeared completely from Hardy's life, though she made a spectacular return in what he described in the *Life* as 'a curious instance of sympathetic telepathy'. In March 1890, on a train journey to London, not knowing that Tryphena was dying, he wrote the first few lines of the poem he later called 'Thoughts of Phena.' [38]. The first stanza of this wistful, elegiac poem is:

> Not a line of her writing have I,
> > Not a thread of her hair,
> Not a mark of her late time as dame in her dwelling, whereby
> > I may picture her there;
> > And in vain do I urge my unsight
> > To conceive my lost prize
> At her close, whom I knew when her dreams were upbrimming
> > with light,
> > And with laughter her eyes.

A case can also be made for his poem 'My Cicely' [31] having been inspired by Tryphena's presence at Topsham. Prompted by news of a loved-one's death, it describes a lover's journey on horseback from London to 'far Exonb'ry'.

> The Nine-Pillared Cromlech, the Bride-streams,
> > The Axe, and the Otter
> I passed, to the gate of the city
> > Where Exe scents the sea.

The 'Nine-Pillared Cromlech' is probably the least well known of the places which the horseman passed. They are the Nine Stones, a mini prehistoric circle that can be seen from your car as you drive west out of Winterbourne Abbas towards Bridport. English Heritage has ensured the conservation of the Nine Stones, but as they are on a bend on a busy main road, with neither walkway nor provision for parking, access is not easy. That Hardy knew of their existence is evidence of how well he knew the archaeology of Dorset.

2. Exeter *(Exonbury)* is the largest cathedral city in the south west of England. In Hardy's short story, 'For Conscience Sake', crusty old bachelor Millborne is driven by his conscience to atone for having abandoned the woman whom he had made pregnant 20 years previously. Now Leonora Frankland, Millborne establishes that she is living with her (and presumably his) daughter in *Exonbury*, where she is a music and dance teacher. He decides to make amends and plans to give her a surprise. Instead, it is Millborne who is surprised. Hardy gives no clues as to where in Exeter he had in mind, if anywhere, for the house in which Mrs Frankland lives and conducts her business.

3. Silverton *(Silverthorn)* A small village just north of Exeter, in the lush valley of the River Exe, *Silverthorn* provides the setting for the longest of Hardy's short stories. 'The Romantic Adventures of a Milkmaid' is the tale of a young lime-burner called Jim and his courtship of the winsome milkmaid Margery. When the melancholic, dark-moustachioed Baron von Xanten becomes infatuated with Margery and sweeps her off to a grand ball, the course of true love is threatened. It is a lively story full of humour, incidents and coincidences. Though they are simple country folk, both Margery and Jim show considerable shrewdness and readiness to turn any situation to their advantage. Margery is tempted by the Baron's offer to leave with him in his yacht, which is harboured at Idmouth (Sidmouth) but in the end chooses Jim.

4. Pilsdon Pen (GR 412012) is a hill in southwest Dorset, crowned with a prehistoric hillfort and panoramic views over three counties and the sea. Its importance to Hardy is evident in 'Wessex Heights' [261], one of his finest poems, written in 1896 when his fiction-writing career was coming to an end and his poetry had not yet taken off. The publication that year of *Jude the Obscure* brought his relationship with Emma to an all-time low point. Only in complete isolation on the Wessex hilltops can he find solace: on Inkpen Beacon, the highest point in England south of the Cotswolds, Wylls-Neck, the highest point in the Quantock Hills, and in Dorset on Bulbarrow and Pilsdon Pen (which in Hardy's day was thought to be the highest point in Dorset)*. Just below, to the west, lies the Marshwood Vale, in which the poem 'A Trampwoman's Tragedy' [153] the four bibulous travellers are 'stung by every Marshwood midge'.

The trampwoman, her fancy-man, jeering John and Mother Lee make their 'toilsome way' to the top of Polden Crest, bound for the 'Marshall's Elm' inn. The trampwoman makes a pass at 'jeering John' and so upsets her 'fancy-man' that when they get to the inn near the summit he murders 'jeering John'.

The Marshwood Vale

* Recent surveys show that the height of Pilsdon Pen is 909 feet (277m) and that of its close neighbour Lewesdon Hill is 915 feet (279m)

The poem begins:

> From Wynyard's Gap the livelong day,
>> The livelong day,
> We beat afoot the northward way
>> We had travelled times before.

Wynyard's Gap (GR 491062) is about six miles to the north east of Pilsdon Pen where there was another inn frequented by the trampwoman and her three friends. The inn also provides a rendez-vous for a seduction in the poem 'At Wynyard's Gap' [718], in which *He* tells *Her* that the view from the top is so good that you can see 'half south Wessex, combe, and glen/ And down, to Lewsdon Hill and Pilsdon Pen.' The Gap and Pilsdon are also mentioned in the poem 'Molly Gone' [444], in which Hardy mourns the death of his sister Mary:

> No more jauntings by Molly and me
>> To the town by the sea,
> Or along over Whitesheet to Wynyard's green Gap,
>> Catching Montacute Crest
> To the right against Sedgemoor, and Corton-Hill's far-distant cap,
>> And Pilsdon and Lewsdon to west.

II - BRIDPORT TO PORTLAND

5. Bridport *(Port-Bredy)* is a town situated west of Dorchester, accessible by the A35, and is the setting for Hardy's short story 'Fellow-Townsmen'. It begins with this description of Port-Bredy (Bridport):

> The shepherd on the east hill could shout out lambing intelligence to the shepherd on the west hill, over the intervening town chimneys, without great inconvenience to his voice, so nearly did the steep pastures encroach upon the burghers' backyards. And at night it was possible to stand in the very midst of the town and hear from the their native paddocks on the lower levels of greensward the mild lowing of the farmer's heifers, and the profound, warm blowings of breath in which those creatures indulge. But the community which

So I am found on Ingpen Beacon, or on Wylls-Neck to the west,
Or else on homely Bulbarrow, or little Pilsdon Crest,
Where men have never cared to haunt, nor women
have walked with me,
And ghosts keep their distance; and I know some liberty.

Pilsdon Pen from the Jurassic Coast

had jammed itself in the valley thus flanked formed a veritable town, with a real mayor and corporation, and a staple manufacture.

Today, driving round Bridport on the by-pass you can clearly see the small hills between which shepherds could swap 'lambing intelligence'. They are a distinctive feature of the surroundings of Bridport. The 'staple manufacture' of the town was, and to a lesser extent still is, rope-making, and there is another reference to it later in the story. To avoid seeing Lucy, the girl he should have married, Barnet takes his walks in the parts of the town away from her house –

> Sometimes he went round by the lower lanes of the borough, where the rope-walks stretched in which his family formerly had share, and looked at the rope-makers walking backwards, overhung by apple-trees and bushes, and intruded on by calves, as if trade had established itself there at considerable inconvenience to Nature.[13]

The community of Port-Bredy has 'jammed itself' into the valley between the hills' - conveying the sense of violating the pastoral world of farming and animals. The trade of rope-making is an intrusion into the natural world of apple-trees and bushes, cows and calves; it is there 'at considerable inconvenience to Nature'.[14] Around and between these references to the rural idyll of a bygone age there unfolds the story of a man who has lost touch with his roots, a 'modern' story of mismatch, misfortune, miscalculation in personal relationships and ultimate unhappiness.

• Bridport is also mentioned in Hardy's 1891 novel, *Tess of the D'Urbervilles*. Eight months after her separation from her husband, Angel Clare, Tess goes to work near *Port-Bredy*:

> After leaving her Marlott home again, she had got through the spring and summer without any great stress upon her physical powers, the time being mainly spent in rendering light irregular service at dairy-work near Port-Bredy, to the west of the Blackmoor Valley, equally remote from her native place and from Talbothays.[15]

6. Netherbury (GR 470994) Three miles to the south west of Beaminster and two miles east of Pilsdon Pen is the village of Netherbury *(Cloton)*. On a road leading to nowhere, it is one of the most beautiful villages

Bridport, West Bay

in Dorset. Netherbury Mill is identifiably the home of Agatha Pollen in Hardy's short story 'Destiny and a Blue Cloak'. (See also Landmark 10).

III – PORTLAND

7. Pennsylvania (Sylvania) Castle. Portland (*The Isle of Slingers* or *Vindilia*) is the predominant setting in Hardy's novel *The Well-Beloved*, which Hardy describes as a 'towering Rock ...a solid and single block of limestone, fully four miles long.' Sylvania Castle is the summer residence of Jocelyn Pierston, a native of the Isle of Slingers, who falls in love with three generations of Avice Caros, in pursuit of ideal love. Adjacent to the castle is Avice's cottage, and from it a lane leads down to Ope (*Hope*) churchyard –

> ...which lay in a ravine formed by a landslip ages ago ...it seemed to say that in this last local stronghold of the Pagan divinities, where Pagan customs lingered yet, Christianity had established itself at best precariously.

Avices's cottage was bought by Dr Marie Stopes, pioneer in birth control, who was a friend of Hardy and his second wife Florence. Stopes rehabilitated the cottage and presented it to the local authority as a museum in 1933. Hardy and Stopes met on many occasions at Dr Stopes' holiday home on Portland – the Old Higher Lighthouse. Another intriguing connection – the two historic cottages linked by two twentieth century giants in their specialist fields.

Portland Museum
(Avice's cottage)

• In *The Well-Beloved* there is a unique moment when Pierston must make a decision about whether or not to marry Avice. When waiting for her to meet him on Chesil Beach he receives a note from Avice informing him that they should be more cautious in their courting, paying respect to the tradition of the isle, and should therefore meet somewhere more populous and not alone. Pierston, frustrated by the traditional behaviour of a girl who he had thought to be 'modern', chooses not to meet her and calls off the engagement:

> ...in such an exposed spot the night wind was gusty, and the sea behind the pebble barrier kicked and flounced in complex rhythms, which could be translated equally well as shocks of battle or shouts of thanksgiving.

Hardy sets this scene of Pierston's emotional confusion upon one of England's most dramatic and unusual coastal formations. Chesil Beach is a prehistoric formation known as a barrier beach, which began to form just after the last ice age, around 14,000 years ago, with huge amounts of shingle being deposited there by the action of marine agents, between 4-5000 years ago. It was entirely appropriate that Hardy should choose it as the setting for the scene in which Pierston's developing feelings for

Avice suddenly dissipate, and yet subliminally continue to accumulate. As the shingle banks of the beach slowly gathered shape and formed over a long period of time, so Pierston's pursuit of his Well-Beloved and her 'many embodiments' continues throughout the book – a search that is motivated by the lost Avice's 'mysterious ingredient sucked from the isle.' The uncertainty and frustration that Pierston experiences on the beach is further suggested by the discordant and intrusive sound of the sea, which carries echoes of 'shocks of battle or shouts of thanksgiving' – figments of Hardy's own imagination which were informed by his historical and archaeological knowledge of the south Dorset coast.

8. Portland Bill *(The Beal)* In Hardy's novel *The Trumpet-Major* it is from the Beal that Ann Garland watches the *Victory* sail past on her way to fight in the Battle of Trafalgar. Anne, from Overcombe (an imaginary mill located somewhere between Upwey and Sutton Poyntz), has to make up her mind between two brothers, John and Bob Loveday. John is the Trumpet-Major and Bob is an officer in the Navy. Eventually she chooses Bob, who achieves his ambition of serving in the *Victory* under Captain Thomas Masterman Hardy, flag-captain to Admiral Lord Nelson. Anne finds out when the *Victory* will be passing down the Dorset coast on its way to Spain and walks all the way from Weymouth to Portland Bill *(Beal)* where she is able to watch the pride of the British Fleet sailing before the wind down the English Channel.

> The great silent ship, with her population of blue-jackets, marines, officers, captain, and the admiral who was not to return alive, passed like a phantom the meridian of the Bill. Sometimes her aspect was that of a large white bat, sometimes that of a grey one. In the course of time the watching girl saw that the ship had passed her nearest point; the breadth of her sails diminished by foreshortening, till she assumed the form of an egg on end.
>
> After this something seemed to twinkle ... the twinkling was the light falling upon the cabin windows of the ship's stern ... The *Victory* was fast dropping away. She was on the horizon, and soon appeared hull down. That seemed to be the beginning of a greater end than her present vanishing.[16]

Lighthouse on Portland Bill

• Nearly thirty years later, Hardy wrote his poem 'The Souls of the Slain' [62], inspired by the beginning of the Crimean War. It is set on Portland Bill where the powerful current known as the Race surges round its southern extremity, usually, it seems, in the direction of Weymouth Bay. It begins:

> The thick lids of Night closed upon me
> Alone at the Bill
> Of the Isle by the Race
> Many-caverned, bald, wrinkled of face -
> And with darkness and silence the spirit was on me
> To brood and be still.

The poet hears the souls of the dead killed in battle returning. They discover that they are not remembered for their heroic deeds but for their acts of humanity. This pleases some of the spirits, who continue homewards, while those of 'bitter tradition' plunged into the Race.

IV – WEYMOUTH (*BUDMOUTH*)

Weymouth is the largest town on the Jurassic Coast and lies eight miles due south of Dorchester. Most of the action in Hardy's novel *The Trumpet-Major* takes place in the Weymouth area, in the years 1804-1808, during the Napoleonic Wars, when King George III and his entourage was a regular visitor there. The focal point of the story is *Overcombe*, the home of the Garlands and the Lovedays, which appears to have been modelled partly on Upwey Mill but located by Hardy in Sutton Poyntz, both of which were then quite separate from the town of Weymouth. There are few Hardy novels in which Weymouth does not feature in some way, and it provides the main setting for a number of his short stories.

9. No. 3, Wooperton Street is the house in Weymouth in which Hardy took lodgings in the early summer of 1869. It was a critical juncture in his life when he was – in his words – 'between architecture and literature'. He had given up his full-time job in London as an architect. He was 29 years of age and unmarried. He had been unsuccessful in his first attempt at a novel – *The Poor Man and the Lady* - and while he got to work on his second attempt – *Desperate Remedies* - he was doing temporary architectural work. Two pictures emerge of Hardy's time in Weymouth, one from the *Life*, the other from what can be gleaned from poems that he wrote during his time in, or about, Weymouth.

In the *Life* he records that he had an interview in Weymouth with the architect G.R. Crickmay for a short-term architectural assignment. After the interview he tells us how, 'with much lightnesss of heart,' he went out onto the Esplanade and, standing in front of the Burdon Hotel, he heard the band playing 'Die Morgenblätter Waltz'; how he used to go for early morning swims, diving from a boat, floating on his back in the sunlit sea; how he went with a friend to dancing classes where he danced with the local girls. It bespeaks a happy, romantic, and fancy-free interlude. By contrast, in a sad poem entitled 'Her Father' [173], a meeting with a girl is spoiled by the presence of her father, though, in recalling the meeting, the poet realises that the father's love for his daughter was enduring, whereas he loved her only for her 'pink and white'. The mother of Tryphena Sparks died in 1868, which supports the claim that the girl is Tryphena. Hardy's poem 'At a

Seaside Town in 1869' [447] portrays the ending of a love affair set amidst the bustle of Weymouth, denoting its popularity as a seaside resort:

> Beyond myself again I ranged
> And saw the free
> Life by the sea,
> And folk indifferent to me.

Whereas in the *Life* Hardy described listening to the Morgenblätter Waltz in the morning, when he was 'facing the beautiful sunlit bay', in the poem he hears the waltz being played in the evening. His poem 'Singing Lovers' [686], written in Weymouth, is also about a lost love. It begins:

> I rowed: the dimpled tide was at the turn,
> And mirth and moonlight spread upon the bay:
> There were two singing lovers in the stern;
> But mine had gone away, -
> Whither, I shunned to say!

Hardy was so successful in destroying all documentary evidence of his private life that we shall never know the truth about his early love life. What we do know is that in March 1870 Hardy was sent on an architectural assignment to St Juliot's in Cornwall, where he met Emma Gifford. On his return he wrote the following poem, titled 'When I set out for Lyonesse' [254]:

> When I set out for Lyonesse
> A hundred miles away,
> The rime was on the spray,
> And starlight in my lonesomeness
> When I set out for Lyonesse
> A hundred miles away.
>
> What should bechance at Lyonesse
> While I should sojourn there
> No prophet durst declare,
> Nor did the wisest wizard guess
> What should bechance at Lyonesse
> While I should sojourn there.

When I came back from Lyonesse
With magic in my eyes,
All marked with mute surprise
My radiance rare and fathomless,
When I came back from Lyonesse
With magic in my eyes!

10. The Esplanade The pride of Weymouth, overlooking the graceful curve of Weymouth Bay, White Nothe and the coast beyond to St. Albans's Head, the Esplanade frequently features in Hardy's work. For example, in *The Trumpet-Major* King George and his family stayed in what was then Gloucester House and later became the Gloucester Hotel; in *Desperate Remedies* Miss Aldcliffe interviews Cytherea in the Belvedere Hotel on the Esplanade; in *Under the Greenwood Tree* Dick Dewey and Fancy Day drive along it.

Weymouth Esplanade

- In Hardy's short story 'Destiny and a Blue Cloak' Agatha Pollin is surprised to find herself walking on the Esplanade with the eligible Oswald Winwood, who has mistaken her for her rival, Frances Lovill. She is about to admit that she is not Frances, but pauses, because he is clearly taken with her.

> The Weymouth season was almost at an end, and but few loungers were to be seen on the parades, particularly at this early hour. Agatha looked over the iridescent sea, from which a veil of mist was slowly rising, at the white cliffs on the left, now just beginning to gleam in a weak sunlight, at the one solitary yacht in the midst, and still delayed her explanation...[17]

Against this beautifully etched background, she makes her ultimately fateful decision.

• The Esplanade also features in the short story 'The History of the Hardcomes', in which first cousins James and Stephen are both engaged to be married, Stephen to Olive and James to Emily. On a whim, at a party after a wedding, they get carried away and agree to change partners. Not until they have got married do they realise that they have made a mistake, but can do nothing about it - until the four of them go on a day's outing to *Budmouth Regis*. At the end of the day they fetch up sitting on the public benches on the Esplanade, listening to the band playing and looking out to sea. Stephen and his sister-in-law Olive both enjoy rowing, whereas Emily and her brother-in-law James do not. So Emily and James remain on the Esplanade and watch Stephen and Olive take a small yellow skiff. Stephen takes the oars and Olive sits opposite him, and Emily and James watch them as they row away, never to return. The next day the little yellow skiff is found drifting bottom up, and the bodies of Stephen and Olive are washed up in *Lulwind Bay* (Lulworth Cove.) 'It was said that they had been found tightly locked in each other's arms, his lips upon hers … "in their death they were not divided"'.

11. The Town Bridge In Hardy's short story 'The Committee-Man of the "Terror"', a middle-aged man arrives in Melcombe Regis by stage-coach at a time when King George III was in town with all the royal court. Seeming to desire obscurity, the man asks directions and proceeds down St. Thomas Street in search of lodgings. He is approaching 'the bridge over the harbour backwater, that then, as now, connected the old portion [Weymouth] with the modern portion [Melcombe Regis]'. A woman of 'twenty-eight or thirty years of age, tall and elegant in figure', is crossing the bridge, coming towards the stranger. She is Mlle V - a French lady who came to live in Weymouth after most of her family had been executed during the Revolution. The sun is shining into the stranger's eyes, so he cannot see her, but with a terrible sense of horror, Mlle V- recognises him as Monsieur G-, a senior official on the 'Committee of Terror' who had authorised the execution. When she faints at his feet from the revulsion of seeing him again he carries her to the nearest shop where she can recover. In spite of her aversion to him, she is attracted to him, and becomes increasingly so as the tragic story unfolds.

12. The Look-out, GR 681783 The Look-out can be found on most street plans of Weymouth, debouching into Newtons Cove on the south side of the Nothe Fort promontory.

In Hardy's short story 'The History of the Hardcomes', when the two couples reach Budmouth-Regis, they go for a walk on the seashore. After looking at the ships in the harbour they go up to the Look-out. (See Hardy landmark no. No. 9, The Esplanade.)

In the short story 'The Melancholy Hussar of the German Legion' it is just by the Look-out that Christoph was due to have a small boat waiting in which he, Matthäus and Phyllis intended to row to France. It all goes tragically wrong. (See Hardy Landmark no. 14)

13. Upwey was once a village on its own quite separate from Weymouth. The old Roman road from Dorchester followed a straight line over the top of the Ridgeway, with its track running from east to west, and through Upwey.

• In Hardy's short story 'A Changed Man' Laura, exiled by her husband to *Creston* (Preston, near Weymouth) during the cholera epidemic, used to meet her lover, Lieut. Vannicock, near the crossing of the old road and the Ridgeway track.

• In *Under the Greenwood Tree* Dick Dewey and Fancy Day stopped off at the Ship Inn which was on the road to the right just below the Ridgeway summit.

• In one of his most exuberant poems, 'Great Things' [414], Hardy celebrates the pleasures of cider-drinking:

> Sweet cyder is a great thing,
>   A great thing to me,
> Spinning down to Weymouth town,
>   By Ridgway thirstily,
> And maid and mistress summoning
>   Who tend the hostelry;
> O cyder is a great thing
>   A great thing to me!

'Spinning down' suggests that Hardy, a keen cyclist, has reached the top of the Ridgeway, and can now take off for Weymouth.

• In stark contrast with 'Great Things', is 'At the Railway Station, Upway' [563], a poignant poem about a convict, a constable and a boy with a violin.

V –WEYMOUTH TO ST. ALDELM'S HEAD
14. Bincombe Church (GR 686845) Hardy started his short story 'The Melancholy Hussar of the German Legion' with this evocative description of Bincombe Down:

> Here stretch the downs, high and breezy and green, absolutely unchanged since those eventful days. A plough has never disturbed the turf, and the sod that was uppermost then is uppermost now.[18]

Sadly this is no longer true. In 2009 it was not ploughs but mechanical diggers which, in an effort to improve the traffic between Dorchester and Weymouth, began work on the controversial Ring Road that irrevocably altered the ancient character of Bincombe Down.

There are entries in the Bincombe Church Parish records (now in the History Centre in Dorchester) for the deaths of Corporal Matth. Tina and Christoph Bless, both of His Majesty's Regiment of German Hussars, shot for desertion and buried on June 30th 1801. These are the facts, coupled with other documentary and hearsay evidence, upon which Hardy based one of his most poignant short stories, 'The Melancholy Hussar of the German Legion.' Matthäus is with the York Hussars of the German Legion, who are serving King George III in defence of the realm against the attack that is anticipated from Napoleon. They are encamped on Bincombe Down above Weymouth. Matthäus, who longs to return to his native Saarbruck, and Phyllis Grove, the daughter of a reclusive doctor, fall in love, even though she is engaged to Humphrey Gould. Matthäus decides to desert and persuades Phyllis to go with him, accompanied by his fellow hussar Christoph. They plan that Christoph will go ahead, steal a small boat moored in Weymouth harbour and row it round the Nothe to a small

Hardy with Bicycle, about 1900 © Dorchester County Museum

inlet. There Matthäus and Phyllis will join him via the Town Bridge and Look-out hill. But Phyllis, torn between love and conscience, decides to remain true to Humphrey Gould. Matthaus and Tina proceed without her. They get as far as Jersey but are caught, sent back and shot for desertion. Phyllis is an involuntary witness of their execution.

15. White Nothe, GR 772807 To the east of Weymouth, White Nothe (the nose) is a headland that projects into the sea between Weymouth Bay and Portland Harbour. The essay by Llewlyn Powys entitled 'The White Nose', begins:

> When I first lived in one of the coastguard cottages on the top of White Nose I was in considerable doubt as to my correct address. As a child I had been taught to refer to the cliff as the White Nore; on the other hand the gate of the coastguard station through which I passed every day presented my eyes with the words White Nothe; while the people of Chaldon Herring were all of them confident that I was living at White Nose. It was this last judgement which eventually won emphatic confirmation from the late Mr Thomas Hardy, who said : "Of course it is White Nose, it always has been called White Nose. You can see if you look that the cliff is shaped like a nose. It is the Duke of Wellington's nose." From that afternoon I have been careful to use the local name.[19]

Despite Hardy's robust claim that it should be White Nose, and Llewelyn Powys's determination to follow the Master, the Ordnance Survey maps of today list the cliff as 'White Nothe.'

16. The Round Pound, GR 796816 The Round Pound, an Iron Age farmstead, is the most prominent and accessible of the archaeological remains which are on the path taken by the smugglers in Hardy's short story 'The Distracted Preacher'; a story described by Arthur McDowall as 'that eventful little comedy which is surely one of the best smuggling stories ever written'.[20] The young Wesleyan Minister, Richard Stockdale, falls in love with Lizzie Newberry, an attractive young widow, who has a share in a smuggling enterprise which operates between *Nether-Moynton* (Owermoigne) and the coast between *Lulwind* (Lulworth) Cove and

Ringsworth (Ringstead). When a lugger with a consignment of brandy arrives from France, the contraband is taken off in small boats and rowed ashore where, under cover of darkness, the smugglers pick it up and carry it back over Chaldon Down to *Nether-Moynton*.

On one smuggling excursion Stockdale and Lizzie leave Nether-Moynton and branch off left before Holworth over Lord's Barrow. At Chaldon they pick up a 'two or three dozen' smugglers. From there, 'leaving East Chaldon on the left' and 'avoiding the cartway', they go over Chaldon Down to 'the crest of a hill at a lonely trackless place not far from the Round Pound earthwork. From there they go to *Dagger's Grave* (Dagger's Gate) 'not many hundred yards from *Lulwind* (Lulworth) Cove,' and then down to 'the verge of the cliff'. There the smugglers drive an iron bar into the ground a yard from the edge and lower a rope to the shore. The rope guides them down to the beach where they unload the brandy from a rowing boat. Each man carries two kegs, 'one on his back, one on his chest, the two being slung together by chords.' This leaves their hands free to pull themselves back up with the help of the rope to the cliff top.

17. Lulworth (*Lulwind*) Cove is best known by Hardy readers as 'the basin of the sea enclosed by the cliffs' where in *Far From the Madding Crowd* Sgt. Troy decides to take a swim.

> Nothing moved in sky, land, or sea, except a frill of milkwhite foam along the nearer angles of the shore, shreds of which licked the contiguous stones like tongues. He descended and came to a small basin of sea enclosed by the cliffs. Troy's nature freshened within him; he thought he would rest and bathe here before going further. He undressed and plunged in. Inside the cove the water was uninteresting to a swimmer, being smooth as a pond, and to get a little of the ocean swell Troy presently swam between the two projecting spurs of rock which formed the pillars of Hercules to this miniature Mediterranean.[21]

As he swims it occurs to him that to fake his own drowning could offer a way out of his loveless marriage and he is presumed dead for a year until he returns.

Lulworth Cove

• Lulworth also features in Hardy's short story 'A Tradition of Eighteen Hundred and Four'. The story is told by Old Solomon Selby who recalls how as a boy watching over the sheep at night with his soldier uncle Job, they witness Bonaparte landing with another officer on a spying expedition. Lulworth is identifiable as 'the three-quarter-round Cove' which in his younger days Old Solomon climbed up 'with two tubs of brandy across my shoulders on scores o' dark nights.'

• In September 1820, the poet Keats, who was on a ship bound for Rome, stopped off at Lulworth Cove where he wrote the sonnet 'Bright star! Would I were as steadfast as thou art!' To mark the centenary Hardy wrote the poem 'At Lulworth Cove a Century Back' [556]. It was a fine tribute to a poet whom Hardy admired – and evidence of what an excellent Poet Laureate Hardy would have made. He was a natural writer of occasional poems, as he had so memorably demonstrated with 'The Convergence of the Twain', subtitled 'Lines on the loss of the Titanic' [248].

18. Encombe House GR 943786 (*Enkworth Court*) is the countryseat of Lord Mountclere in Hardy's novel *The Hand of Ethelberta*. Lord Mountclere invites Ethelberta to a party there, at which, in her capacity as professional story-teller, she tells the true story of her life. Knowing that he knows the truth about her background, Ethelberta accepts his proposal of marriage.

Describing the house, Hardy wrote:

> Without attempting an analogy between a man and his mansion, it may be stated that everything here, though so dignified and magnificent, was not conceived in quite the true and eternal spirit of art. It was a house in which Pugin would have torn his hair. Those massive blocks of red-veined marble, lining the hall – emulating in their surface glitter the Escalier de Marbre at Versailles - were cunning imitations in paste and plaster by workmen brought from afar for the purpose.[22]

(see also Landmark No. 20, West End Cottage).

VI - ST ALDHELM'S HEAD TO OLD HARRY ROCKS

19. West End Cottage, Swanage (*Knollsea*), GR 032785 Hardy married Emma Gifford on 17th September 1874. Returning from their honeymoon in France, they lived first at Surbiton and then off Westbourne Grove, London. Despite the success of *Far From the Madding Crowd* the future was uncertain, not least where they would live. They were evidently considering somewhere in the Purbeck area, and for a short while stayed in lodgings in Bournemouth. Emma recorded in her diary that on St Swithin's Day they took the steamer to Swanage and took a room for the night in West End Cottage in what was then Royal Victoria Road, now Seymer Road. Hardy's poem 'We Sat at the Window' [355], sub-titled 'Bournemouth, 1875', indicates that after less than a year of marriage Hardy and Emma were having problems:

> We sat at the window looking out,
> And the rain came down like silken strings
> That Swithin's day. Each gutter and spout
> Babbled unchecked in the busy way
>   Of witless things:
> Nothing to read, nothing to see
> Seemed in that room for her and me
>   On Swithin's day.

We were irked by the scene, by our own selves; yes.
For I did no know, nor did she infer
How much there was to read and guess
By her in me, and to see and crown
    By me in her.
Wasted were two souls in their prime,
And great was the waste, that July time
    When the rain came down.

Biographers differ over how seriously things had gone wrong at this early stage in their marriage and the poem should be viewed in context. Relations with both sets of 'in-laws' were strained and neither had seen many old friends since their marriage. In his autobiography Hardy says 'they found lodgings at the house of an invalided captain of smacks and ketches.'[23] This was Captain Masters and his wife, whose household provided the peace and security Hardy needed for completing his fifth novel, *The Hand of Ethelberta*, which was well under way by the time the Hardys moved to Swanage. Captain Masters features in the novel as Captain Flowers. Hardy described *Knollsea* as –

> a seaside village lying snug within two headlands as between a finger and thumb. Everybody in the parish who was not a boatman was a quarrier, unless he were the gentleman who owned half the property and had been a quarryman, or the other gentleman who owned the other half, and had been to sea.

> The knowledge of the inhabitants was of the same special sort as their pursuits. The quarrymen in white fustian understood practical geology, the laws and accidents of dips, faults, and cleavage, far better than the ways of the world and mammon; the seafaring men in Guernsey frocks had a clearer notion of Alexandria, Constantinople, the Cape, and the Indies than of any inland town in their own country. This, for them, consisted of a busy portion, the Channel, where they lived and laboured, and a dull portion, the vague unexplored miles of interior at the back of the ports, which they seldom thought of.[24]

Also associated with Hardy's Swanage interlude is the poem 'The Sunshade' [434], of which the first and last stanzas are given here.

> Ah – it's the skeleton of a lady's sunshade,
>   Here at my feet in the hard rock's chink,
>   Merely a naked sheaf of wires!-
>   Twenty years have gone with their livers and diers
>   Since it was silked in its white or pink.

> Is the fair woman who carried that sunshade
>   A skeleton just as her property is,
>   Laid in the chink that none may scan?
>   And does she regret – if regret dust can –
>   The vain things thought when she flourished this.

20. Durlston Head, GR 036772 Durlston Head is a large headland above Durlston Bay, which became a renowned site for Lower Cretaceous fossils in the 1850s after the discovery of a mammal jaw by Samuel Beckles. In 1857 Beckles directed one of the greatest excavations there of fossil mammals, known as 'Beckles Pit'. In *The Hand of Ethelberta*, the heroine first lodges with her brothers and sisters at West End Cottage, but then moves up-market to a brand-new 'porticoed and balconied dwelling' suitable for her to be visited by Lord Mountclere. It is thought that Hardy had in mind one of the houses built by Mr George Burt when Swanage was becoming a popular holiday resort.[25] Hardy later met Burt in 1892, when he and Emma visited Swanage on a Field-Club meeting.[26] Burt conducted the party to Durlston Head where they had lunch in the 'handsome restaurant at the summit of the Head' (as reported in the *Dorset County Chronicle*).

• Hardy recorded in his autobiography that during their stay at West End Cottage (1875-1876) he and Emma 'walked daily on the cliffs and shore'.[27] Durlston Head is one mile south of West End Cottage. One autumn evening Hardy made the following note:

> Just after sunset. Sitting with E. on a stone under the wall before the Refreshment Cottage.* The sounds are two, and only two. On the

---

* The Refreshment Cottage became first Belle View Restaurant, and later Tilly Whim Inn, before demolition.

left Durlstone [sic] Head roaring high and low, like a giant asleep. On the right a thrush. Above the bird hangs the new moon, and a steady planet.[28]

• Hardy wrote two poems in which Durlston Head features, both of which were published in 1925. In the first, 'Once at Swanage' [753], he refers again to the sound of the sea in the second verse:

> Roaring high and roaring low was the sea
>> Behind the headland shore
>> It symboled the slamming of doors
> Or a regiment hurrying over hollow floors. . . .
>> And there we two stood, hands clasped; I and she!

The second poem, 'To a Sea-Cliff'' (sub-titled 'Durlston Head') [768] denotes particularly well Hardy's affinity with the Jurassic Coast. The poem explores the relationship between history and geology – between the emotional human past and the enduring indifference of the stone – which both awed and alienated Hardy's poetic imagination:

'To a sea-cliff'

Lend me an ear
While I read you here
A page from your history,
Old cliff – not known
To your solid stone,
Yet yours inseparably.

Endnotes

1. Information taken from the official website of the Jurassic Coast. Available online from: www.jurassiccoast.com

2. Information correct at the time of writing.

3. The *Times*, July 9th 1910.

4 *The Poetry of Thomas Hardy: A Handbook and Commentary.* by Bailey, J.O, pub. University of North Carolina Press: Chapel Hill, 1970, p.345.

5. *Life,* p.401.

6. Ibid, p.25.

7. *Thomas Hardy: A Biography Revisted*, Michael Millgate, Oxford University Press 2004, p. 359.

8. Ibid, p.81 and p.82.

9. See *Brewers Dictionary of Phrase and Fable* 1974, pub. Cassell & Company Ltd., p.234.

10. *The Well-Beloved*, New Wessex edition, p. 34.

11. *Introduction to the Ethnology of Dorset, and other Archaeological Notices of the County*, Wake Smart, William, pub. Bournemouth: D. Sydenham, 1872, pp.277-308.

12. See commentary on Barnes' article in 'Minor Correspondence', Gentleman's Magazine, (1839:Feb.) p.114.

13. *Thomas Hardy: Collected Short Stories*. New Wessex. Macmillan Papermac 1988. 'Fellow-Towsmen', p.79.

14. Ibid, p.90.

15. *Tess of the d'Urbervilles.* Edited by Juliet Grindle and Simon Gatrell, Oxford University Press. Oxford. 1988, p.266.

16. From chapter 34 of The Trumpet-Major.

17. *Thomas Hardy: Collected Short Stories*. New Wessex Edition, Macmillan Papermac 1988, p.880.

18. 'The Melancholy Hussar'. Thomas Hardy: Collected Short Stories. New Wessex Edition, Macmillan Papermac 1988, p.35.

19. P.1, Dorset Essays, pub. John Lane the Bodley Head, 1935, p.1.

20. *Thomas Hardy: A Critical Study*, Arthur McDowall, London, 1933, Faber & Faber, p.59.

21. From chapter 47 of Far From the Madding Crowd.

22. From chapter 38 of The Hand of Ethelberta.

23. Ibid, p.110.

24. From Chapter 31 of The Hand of Ethelberta.

25. 'Thomas Hardy's Winter Stay in Swanage'. In *Thomas Hardy Year Book*. David Lewer, 1970, Toucan Press, Guernsey, pp.45-7.

26. *Life,* p.263.

27. Ibid, p.111.

28. Ibid, p.111.

THE THOMAS HARDY SOCIETY

The Society aims to promote the work of Thomas Hardy for both education and enjoyment. Members include scholars, students, readers, and enthusiasts - anyone with an interest in his poetry, novels, short stories or in his life and times. The Society runs a weeklong biennial international conference, organises tours and walks in Wessex, and publishes three journals a year.

To learn more about the Society, or to join, visit our website www.hardysociety.org or write to us at The Thomas Hardy Society, c/o The Dorset County Museum, High West Street, Dorchester, Dorset. DT1 1SD, or email us at info@hardysociety.org

THE COMPILERS

Patrick Tolfree has been a freelance writer for the past 20 years, his previous career having been in industry. His special interest is Hardy's short stories. Patrick is a Vice-President of the Thomas Hardy Society and lives in Dorchester.

Rebecca Welshman is a freelance writer and research assistant at the University of Exeter. She is writing a PhD titled 'Imagining Archaeology', which considers the role of archaeology in the work of Thomas Hardy and Richard Jefferies. Rebecca is the student representative on the Thomas Hardy Society Council of Management and lives in Somerset.

THE ILLUSTRATOR

David Brackston is a professional landscape artist. He was educated at the Hardy School in Dorchester, and now lives in Somerset. The featured illustrations, along with David's other work, can be viewed at: www.brax.org.uk To contact David directly please write to: David Brackston, Cobwebs, North Street, Crewkerne, Somerset. TA187AJ. Email: david@brax.org.uk

THE JURASSIC COAST TRUST

The Jurassic Coast Trust is an independent charity working with partners to support World Heritage education, conservation, science and arts programmes for the benefit of all – now and in the future. For more details see: www.jurassiccoasttrust.org

PORTLAND MUSEUM

The Museum was founded by Dr Marie Stopes for the sole purpose of providing a "community museum" for the people of the Island of Portland. Dr Stopes purchased the two historic cottages that made up the original museum and gifted them in perpetuity to the Islanders in 1930. Portland Museum Trust, a registered charity, was formed in June 2007 to take over operational and managerial responsibility for Portland Museum, which hitherto had been run by Weymouth & Portland Borough Council.